The Sleepover Club

Have you been invited to all these sleepovers?

Sleepover Girls go Treasure Hunting

by Sue Mongredien

Collins

An imprint of HarperCollins*Publishers*

For Hannah and Tom – my own little treasures

The Sleepover Club ® is a
registered trademark of HarperCollins*Publishers* Ltd

First published in Great Britain by Collins in 2003
Collins is an imprint of HarperCollins*Publishers* Ltd
77-85 Fulham Palace Road, Hammersmith,
London W6 8JB

The HarperCollins website address is
www.**fire**and**water**.com

1 3 5 7 9 8 6 4 2

Text copyright © Sue Mongredien 2003

Original series characters, plotlines
and settings © Rose Impey 1997

ISBN 0 00 711772 8

The author asserts the moral right to
be identified as the author of the work.

Printed and bound in England by
Clays Ltd, St Ives plc

Sleepover Kit List

1. Sleeping bag
2. Pillow
3. Pyjamas or a nightdress
4. Slippers
5. Toothbrush, toothpaste, soap etc
6. Towel
7. Teddy
8. A creepy story
9. Food for a midnight feast:
   chocolate, crisps, sweets, biscuits.
   In fact anything you like to eat.
10. Torch
11. Hairbrush
12. Hair things like a bobble or hairband,
    if you need them
13. Clean knickers and socks
14. Change of clothes for the next day
15. Sleepover diary and membership card

CHAPTER ONE

Hello! Lyndz here. How are you? I don't suppose you've got a bit of time to hear about how the Sleepover Club went treasure hunting, have you? Oh, good! Come into the garden and we can sit on the swings while I tell you all about it.

The rest of the Sleepover lot thought I should be the one to tell you the story of our treasure-hunting adventures seeing as it all started off right here, in the garden. See the big ash tree over there? Well, that's where Buster...

Oh. I haven't even introduced you to

Buster! He's our dog. Do you like dogs? Even people who aren't really into animals, i.e. Fliss, end up liking Buster because he's so funny and friendly and GORGEOUS! He's our Jack Russell terrier and has always got his little nose into something or other.

It was actually Buster's cute little button nose that started us off on our search for treasure this time. Let me tell you how it all happened.

It was Saturday morning and the five of us – that's me, Rosie, Frankie, Kenny and Fliss – were sitting around the breakfast table at my house. We'd just had an awesome Sleepover the night before and were giggling about Fliss's sleep talking which had woken all of us up through the night.

"You were saying something about having your hair cut, I think," Rosie said, spreading marmalade on her toast. "You definitely said something about your fringe anyway."

"Yeah, and I heard you say, 'Shave it all off please – give me the baldy look!'" Kenny joked. (If you didn't know, Kenny is the biggest wind-up merchant in the world. Don't believe ANYTHING she tells you!)

Fliss squealed and clapped her hands onto her long, blonde hair at once. Even though she's known Kenny from the first day we were at primary school together, she still falls for Kenny's wind-ups every time. "There's no way in the world I'd have said that, Kenny," she said seriously. "Unless I was having a nightmare!"

The rest of us chuckled. "I dunno – I think a skinhead might suit you," Frankie said thoughtfully. "What do you reckon, girls?"

"Noooooo!" Fliss squeaked in horror. "Don't even SAY that word to me!"

"They're only kidding you," I told Fliss, patting her arm. "I never heard you say anything about getting your head shaved anyway. When I heard you, you were muttering about mashed potato!"

"Ooh, was I?" Fliss said. "That's because my mum's on a diet again and we're not allowed to have any potatoes in the house. Or biscuits. Or chocolates. Or cakes. Or cheese. Or..."

"And out of all those things, mashed potato is what you miss the most?" Frankie asked, raising an eyebrow. "You freak!"

"Oooh, but come on, though... soft, fluffy mash..." Fliss said dreamily, with a faraway look in her eyes. "I could eat it for breakfast!"

My mum was buttering some more toast for us and laughed at those words. "Fliss, I don't have time to do you some mash for breakfast but if you stick around for lunch, I'll make sure there's some on the table," she said. "How does that sound?"

Fliss went a bit pink. She always goes a bit funny and shy around other people's mums and dads. "Thank you, Mrs Collins," she said politely. "That's really REALLY kind of you!"

Mum laughed again, Fliss was sounding so thrilled. "Glad to help out," she said. "Same goes for the rest of you if you want to stay for veggie sausages and mash?"

Even though we were all stuffed with toast and marmalade and boiled eggs and porridge at this point, every single one of us said, "Yes, PLEASE!" as if we hadn't been fed for six weeks. The Sleepover Club have biiiig appetites!

After breakfast, we went outside to mess about in the garden with Buster. It was a really sunny day and before long, we were running off our big breakfasts with a game of leapfrog. Our garden is quite long and wide so we were able to keep leapfrogging around in a big circle. Buster got all excited and kept running round our legs until I got worried he was going to get jumped on, and moved him out of the way.

Buster was a bit put out by that, I think – he hates being left out of anything, especially a game that involves lots of running around – but obediently trotted off to do one of his favourite things, which is sniffing around the flowerbeds.

If you've got a dog yourself, you'll know all about the sniffing thing. They just can't resist having a good old sniff of anything they come across – in the street, in the park, even in your own garden when they've sniffed it a million times already! Still, it just goes to show that dogs must know something we don't know because it was Buster's sniffing that started us off on the treasure hunt. He must have sniffed around our garden a gazillion times by now and never found much that was interesting – the odd bone, a dead mouse one of the cats had caught, some compost – you know, nothing more exciting than that... but today, all that sniffing paid off.

WOOF! WOOF!

If you've got a dog, you'll also know that different woofs mean different things. Big, deep woofs are to try and sound scary when the postman is at the door. Short, high-pitched woofs are more of an excited noise. And from all the yapping he was doing at the other end of the garden, I knew he was all worked up about something or other.

"Oof!" Kenny finished her round of leapfrogs, and we all stopped to watch Buster. He was scrabbling away in the soil and kept cocking his head at me and barking louder and louder.

"I think he's saying we should be playing leap*dog*, not leapfrog," Rosie joked.

"Oh, I hope he hasn't found a real frog

from next door's pond," I said, feeling worried. "He's got a real thing about them and I'm sure they don't think it's such good fun when he tries to play with them."

"Frogs, YUCK!" Fliss said at once. She is one of those people who feels sick at the thought of blood, beetles, spiders, snakes, rats, mud, bad smells, ghosts, dead things... you get the idea.

"Oh, frogs are sooo sweet," I said defensively. "How can you not like a cute little froggy, Fliss?" I didn't bother to wait for her answer – I didn't have time to listen to all the reasons she would be able to come up with for hating them. "Hang on – I'll just see what he's found."

I ran off up the garden, half hoping it really was a frog but thinking that, more likely, it was going to be a worm or piece of rubbish that the wind had blown in. I certainly wasn't expecting to find some treasure!

As I got near him, Buster started running round and round in circles, barking dementedly. "Calm down, daft dog!" I said, laughing.

13

He ran over to something he'd uncovered in the soil and pushed it with his nose. It glinted gold in the autumn sun.

"What have you found, then?" I said. I still wasn't excited at this point, I was just wondering if it was a shiny chocolate wrapper (not that I have food on the brain or anything!). It wasn't until I got right there and bent over to look that I realised that it wasn't just a piece of old rubbish. Oh, no! Quite the opposite, in fact. Buster had found... a gold ring.

"Buster, where did this come from?" I asked in surprise. I picked up the ring and blew the last crumbs of soil off it. It felt heavy and warm in my hand.

"Hey, look at this, you guys," I shouted excitedly. "Buster has struck GOLD!"

The other four ran over to have a look. "Wow! A ring! Where do you think it came from?" Fliss said, eyes wide. "Can I try it on?"

"Is it one of your mum's rings?" practical Rosie said. "Or yours?"

"It's not mine and I don't think it's Mum's," I replied. "I've never seen it before."

"Is it your dad's?" Kenny asked. "Or one of your brothers'? It must have come from *somewhere*."

Fliss rolled her eyes. "Honestly, Kenny, don't you know anything about jewellery? It's a lady's ring – look how small it is!" she said, wiggling her middle finger which was now wearing the ring. Fliss is very into stuff like jewellery and make-up – and she also loves a chance to go on about it whenever possible.

"No, I didn't know because I'm not interested," Kenny retorted, quick as a flash. "And anyone who IS interested must be..."

"Hey, I wonder if it's something to do with the supernatural," Frankie interrupted. Out of the five of us, Kenny and Fliss are the ones who argue most often, so Rosie, Frankie and I have to jump in and stop them before it gets out of hand. "I mean, things don't just *appear* in people's gardens like that, do they? It could be a sign!" she added, looking excited.

"Supernatural?" scoffed Rosie at once. "Sign? Leave it out, Frankie. It's a ring that Buster has found, that's all."

"Now, don't look like that," Frankie said. "I saw this wicked episode of the *X-Files* once, where..."

"Here we go..." muttered Kenny, raising her eyebrows at Rosie. Those two don't have *any* time for Frankie's theories about aliens, UFOs and spaceships. The drama with Frankie's telescope and 'alien' spotting on Cuddington Hill was something we were still trying to live down. "Now – getting back to the real world, has anyone been doing any digging in the garden lately?" she added loudly, drowning out Frankie's *X-Files* story.

I wrinkled my nose while I thought. "Yes, Mum was out here last weekend," I said. "She roped me into helping her with the weeding. Why?"

"Well... DERRR!" Kenny said, her face lighting up. "Hasn't it struck anyone else what the obvious answer is?"

The rest of us looked at each other blankly. "Er... a magic plant that grows gold rings?" Fliss said feebly.

Rosie giggled. "Fliss, you've been reading

too much Enid Blyton," she said. "Magic plant, indeed!"

"I'm talking about buried treasure, you dimwits!" Kenny said dramatically. "I bet when your mum was digging over her flowerbeds, she dug this ring up without even realising. Which means that..."

"There could be more down there," Rosie put in, grabbing Kenny's arm excitedly. "Buried treasure – in your garden, Lyndz!"

"From years and years ago," Kenny added, eyes gleaming. "It's probably really REALLY old and dead valuable."

Even Fliss had stopped glaring at Rosie and was looking interested now. "What, you mean, we could be rich?" she said eagerly.

"Could be!" I said, grinning at her. I started skipping back towards the house. "Come on, let's go and show my mum what we've found!"

CHAPTER TWO

You know what it's like when you're dead excited about something and then you show your parents and they're like, "Oh yeah, whatever," as if they've just seen the most boring thing on earth? Well, that was kind of what I was expecting to happen with the ring as well – for Mum and Dad to crush our excitement with lots of boring, practical reasons why we couldn't possibly have found some real treasure.

Which just goes to show that parents are totally unpredictable creatures because – miracle of the year – they didn't say anything of the sort.

"Mum, look what Buster found in the garden," I shouted as we went into the kitchen. Mum and Dad were both there reading the newspaper and trying to stop my baby brother Spike ripping up the TV guide.

Fliss wiggled the ring off her finger and dropped it into my mum's hand. "Treasure!" she beamed.

"Is it yours, Mrs Collins?" Sherlock Kenny wanted to know at once. "Did you lose it when you were gardening?"

Mum shook her head. "No, it's not one of mine," she said, peering at it. "I've never seen it before. It's very pretty. I wonder whose it is."

"We were wondering if there could be some buried treasure in the garden," I burst out excitedly. "What do you think? You might have dug this up the other day when we were out in the garden – and there might be loads more where it came from, too!"

Fliss sat down at the kitchen table suddenly, looking really pale and scared. "I've just had a horrible thought," she said faintly. "What if there's a dead body down there? A dead body that was WEARING THE RING!"

"Eeeeuughh, do you have to, Fliss?" Rosie said. "Thanks for that lovely idea – not!"

"Darling, I'm sure if I'd raked over the hand of a dead woman, I'd have noticed," Mum said calmly. She is not the tiniest bit squeamish – as you probably guessed.

"Raked over the... ugh," Fliss echoed, her face changing from white to green in seconds. She clapped a hand over her mouth and looked sick as anything. "I wish you hadn't said that, Mrs Collins."

Dad took the ring out of Mum's hand and examined it. "It feels heavy enough to be real gold," he said, sounding interested. "Whereabouts did you find it?"

"Near the ash tree," I said. "Can we go and do some digging there to see what else we can find, please, please, PLEASE?"

"Definitely not," Mum said at once. "I can just see it now – my rose bushes all destroyed by you five, hacking away at their roots. No, thank you very much!"

"Oh, per-leeeeze, Mum," I wheedled. "We'd be dead careful."

"I mean, if it really is buried treasure, there's bound to be more down there, isn't there?" Kenny reasoned. "After all, no one would bury a single ring, would they?"

"It'll be just like *Time Team*!" Frankie piped up. "I saw it the other week, right, and they'd found this whole Roman campground that they were digging up. It was soooo cool. They found bits of old Roman wine goblets and parts of old spears and all sorts of cool stuff!"

"Awesome," Kenny said. "Hey – what if Romans used to live here in your village, Lyndz?"

"What if they lived in your HOUSE?" Fliss breathed excitedly.

My dad burst out laughing. "As this is a Victorian house, I doubt it," he chuckled. "Fliss, remind me – what century is this again?"

Fliss frowned at him. "Is this a trick question?" she asked suspiciously. "It's the 21st century of course!"

"Right," Dad said. "And the Romans were around... when?"

Fliss shrugged. "Erm... about a hundred years ago?" she guessed, looking uncomfortable.

"The Romans were around in the FIRST century," Dad told her. "Nearly two THOUSAND years ago. Now, I know our house might look two thousand years old, but..." he joked.

"Dad, do you think this ring could be two thousand years old?" I asked excitedly. "How old might it be?"

Dad peered at it again. "It's hard to say with gold," he said, shaking his head. "It ages very well. I very much doubt it's Roman though, but..."

"Just think, if we DID find a whole hoard of Roman treasure, we'd be famous," Rosie said dreamily, completely ignoring my dad. "We'd be on the news and everything."

"And rich," I said pointedly. "Weren't you saying the other night, Mum, that you didn't know how you were going to pay for the loft extension?"

"Lyndsey, I don't think your friends need to hear about our money problems," Mum said with an edge in her voice. She gave me a sharp look over the top of her glasses which said, clear as day, Shut up, Lyndz.

I closed my mouth and looked down. When my mum gives you THAT look, you know it's best not to argue. But why is it that parents go all weird when you start talking about money? When I'm grown up, I won't care about how much people earn or how much someone's house is worth – who's interested, anyway? I've noticed that grown-ups get dead twitchy and secretive about it though. Odd, isn't it? You'd think they could find something more interesting to get their knickers in a twist over.

I was just starting to think that was going to be the end of any treasure hunting, there and then, when my dad cleared his throat. "Well, maybe it would be worth having another quick look around the ash tree," he said slowly. "A SUPERVISED quick look under the tree so that no one does any damage to the rose bushes. Or their roots," he added quickly before my mum could say it.

"YEAHHHH!" I yelled.

"Yay!", "Result!", "Nice one, Mr C!" the others cheered.

Mum still didn't look too thrilled at the idea of us digging up the garden. "Keith, I mean it – if anybody digs up anything they shouldn't, I really will not be happy..." she said to my dad warningly, as she started tidying up the newspapers and Spike's toys.

"Don't worry," Dad said. "You won't even know we've been there. Apart from the huge heap of gold coins and goodies we're going to bring back with us, of course..."

"WHOOOPEEEE!" Kenny yelled, bouncing around the kitchen like a mad jack-in-a-box. "Come on – let's go and dig up that booty – like, NOW!"

"Clever, clever Buster," I said, stooping down to pat him proudly. "We're going to be rich and famous – all because of you. You'll get the biggest, juiciest steak there ever was for being such a good little treasure hunter."

Mum rolled her eyes. "Now, don't go making promises you can't afford to keep, Lyndz," she said, as we went out the back door.

Luckily, Dad was a bit keener on the idea of treasure than Mum was. He once told me his favourite book when he was a boy was *Treasure Island*, so he was getting well into the idea. "Right, girls, let's sort out some digging tools," he said, rubbing his hands. "Follow me to the shed and we'll see what we can find."

Minutes later, we were "all tooled up" as Dad put it. He had Mum's garden spade, I had my brother Stu's smaller spade, Kenny and Frankie had trowels and Rosie and Fliss drew the short straw and had to make do with plastic beach spades. "I've never seen the *Time Team* people using bright pink and yellow spades before!" Rosie joked as we went over to the tree.

"That's 'cos we're the cool new version of *Time Team*," Frankie said. "Treasure Team!"

Dad chuckled. "Right then, Treasure Team – where did Buster dig up this 'ere 'ighly valuable piece of gold?" he asked.

"Just there," I said, crouching down and pointing. "See his scratch marks?"

"You know what, if we really ARE going to be like *Time Team*, we're going to have to be very careful," Fliss said solemnly. "They just scrape away at the soil dead gently, don't they, so they don't damage or scratch any of the buried treasure in the ground."

"Oh, let's just get on with it and get stuck into the digging," Kenny said impatiently, and then remembered my mum's warning. "Er... Very carefully, of course..."

"Fliss, if by any remote chance there does happen to be Roman treasure down there, we'll be scraping away at the soil for weeks before we get to it," Dad pointed out. "It won't be lying just under the surface, will it?"

"And remember, Mum's just dug up loads of this flowerbed and she wasn't scraping gently at all," I added. "So it might be a bit late to start all that now."

"All right, all right," Fliss said huffily, her cheeks going a bit pink. "I just think, if we're going to do this, we may as well do it properly, that's all, but if you all think you know better, then..."

"Let's get going, then," Frankie said, before Fliss could get too carried away. "And anything we find gets split equally, yeah?"

"After we've bought Buster's steak, yeah," I agreed. "Let's get to work!"

So the great garden dig-up began. At first, we were all dead excited about what we might find, and started talking about what we'd spend our riches on. Fliss was going to have a wild shopping weekend in London with her mum (of course). Kenny fancied an adventure holiday bungee jumping and snowboarding in New Zealand. I was going to set up an animal welfare centre. Rosie wanted to buy a posh new house for her mum and Frankie was going to take her family on holiday to Florida so she could go to the Epcot Centre and the NASA space station. Dad said he was going to take Mum away on a romantic holiday and leave us kids to fend for ourselves for a few weeks. I *think* he was joking...

Then a scream came from Fliss. "Oh, oh, ugh, GROSS!!" she squealed, dropping her spade as if it was burning hot, and leaping away.

"What's up? Is it the dead woman's hand?" Kenny asked eagerly, coming to have a look at what Fliss had found.

Fliss shuddered and closed her eyes. "A worm! A worm!" she moaned dramatically. "It was wriggling on my spade and everything!"

"Oh, FLISS," I said, going over to pick it up. "You've probably scared it by screaming like that, poor little thing."

"Do you reckon?" Rosie asked, sounding interested. "Do worms have ears, then?"

The others looked at me, expecting me to know but I had no idea. "Well, I can't *see* any," I said, peering doubtfully at the pink wriggler in my hand.

"That reminds me," Kenny giggled. "What did the earwig say as he crawled into Fliss's ear?"

"Kenny!" Fliss groaned, shaking her head and looking sick again. "Please just... shut up!"

"Earwig-o, earwig-o, earwig-o," Kenny sang. "Geddit? 'Ere we go, 'ere we go, 'ere we go...'"

"You're lucky I'm too scared to touch that worm," Fliss said, sounding fierce. "Else I might just have dropped it down your neck for that, Kenny McKenzie. I'm going to have nightmares about earwigs crawling into my brain now, thank you very much."

"How about this one?" Frankie said, with a mischievous glint in her eye. "There's a worm at the bottom of the garden and his name is Wiggly-Woo..."

The rest of us immediately joined in the song.

"There's a worm at the bottom of the garden
And all that he can do
Is wiggle all night and wiggle all day..."

"Stop it!" wailed Fliss.

"Come on, Fliss," my dad said, seeing her bottom lip sticking out about ten centimetres. "Ignore them. Think about all those clothes you're going to buy, eh?"

We were all in a silly mood by then. "I've just dug up a pop group," Rosie giggled. "Look – it's the beetles!"

Even Fliss laughed at that. "Hey, I've got one – what's a gardener's favourite Christmas carol?" she said, joining in. "Soil-ent night!"

Soon we were all coming out with them.

"What smells most in the garden?" Dad asked. "Your nose!"

"Where do insects live?" Frankie said. "Crawley!"

We were having such a laugh, I couldn't believe it was lunch time already when I heard Mum calling us. Treasure hunting was turning out to be the best fun we'd had in aaaaages!

CHAPTER THREE

After a whopping great lunch of bangers and mash – with Fliss having THIRDS of mash – digging up the garden suddenly didn't seem like so much fun any more.

"I've got blisters from that spade," I said, holding my hands out for the others to see.

"My hands are a bit sore as well," Fliss said at once. "Has anybody got any hand cream on them?"

"And we haven't found ANYTHING except worms and beetles and centipedes," Rosie said, sounding disappointed.

"Hey, what happened to the rich and famous Treasure Team?" Dad said, trying to jolly us along a bit. "Not giving up already, are you? We've hardly started!"

"Mr C, you're a much better digger than we are," crafty Kenny started. "I don't suppose you'd fancy..."

"What, finishing off the digging all by myself?" Dad said, raising his eyebrows. "I didn't think the Sleepover Club were the sort to be so lazy as to ask a poor, tired old man who's been working hard all week to give up his Saturday afternoon to..."

"All right, all right, Dad!" I interrupted hurriedly. "No need to give us the sob story."

Mum cleared our plates away and we sat around the table looking at each other. "So does ANYONE fancy digging some more?" I asked in the end. Even though I wanted to find buried treasure as badly as everyone else, my blisters really were throbbing on my hand – and suddenly, I could think of lots of other things I'd rather be doing than digging up the flowerbed all afternoon.

"I've got to meet my mum – we're going to the library," Rosie said. "Otherwise I'd stay and help, of course..."

"And my mum's having some people round this afternoon and I said I'd help look after baby Izzy while she gets things ready," Frankie added. "So I'm going to have to shoot off soon, too."

"I promised I'd clean out Merlin's cage," Kenny said. "He's getting a bit whiffy and Mum's been threatening to let next door's dog have him if I don't de-pong him soon."

"She wouldn't!" I cried in horror. Merlin is Kenny's pet rat that she's taught to do all sorts of tricks. The thought of letting him be eaten by the dog next door was just...

"No, she wouldn't," Kenny agreed. "She was just trying to make me feel bad – and it worked, as usual."

"But what about our treasure?" Fliss put in. "Mr Collins is right. We can't give up already. I want my shopping trip to London soooo badly! I've been thinking about all the things I want to buy."

I was just about to invite her to carry on digging, but she must have second-guessed me, because before I could open my mouth...

"Obviously, I'd stay and help you dig up the garden, Lyndz and Mr Collins, but I... er... I've got to get back, too. Mum's got... er... something planned. Unfortunately," she said quickly. She tossed her head and looked around the table, daring anyone to question her.

"So we all want the treasure but nobody wants to dig any more, that's about the size of it," I summarised. "Well, what do we do next, then?"

"I could have a look in the library for ideas," Rosie offered. "See if I can find anything about Roman settlements around here in the local history section. We might get some clues from that."

"Good idea," Kenny said. "See if you can find a map that says where all the Roman ruins are around the country and which are the nearest to us."

"There are some in Bath," Fliss put in helpfully. "I know, because Andy used to live there and he told me."

"Yeah, but that's miles away," Kenny said, unimpressed. "It's not like a Roman soldier would pop out here to Little Wearing for the day all the way from Bath, is it?"

Fliss looked cross. "I was just SAYING," she retorted. "Anyway, Little Wearing might be on the WAY from Bath to somewhere else. Soldiers could have camped here overnight, couldn't they? Or didn't you think of that, Miss Smarty-Pants?"

"Oooooooh!" Kenny said sarcastically. "Get you, Miss University Challenge!"

"Hey!" Frankie yelled suddenly, interrupting the bickering. "I've just had the most WICKED idea. My uncle's got a metal detector – why don't I ask if we can borrow that for our treasure hunting? We can just sweep it around Lyndz's garden to see if there IS anything metal buried there – and we won't have to do any more digging!"

"Sounds a wonderful idea," Mum said at once. "And then my roses might actually get to live to see next summer!"

"A metal detector – COOL," Kenny breathed happily. "I've always wanted to have a go with one. Do you think he would lend it to us?"

"Oh, yeah, totally," Frankie said, sounding confident. "He's the one who gave me the telescope, remember? My cousins – his kids – are soooo not into stuff like that, and he's always dead keen for me to have a go with all his weird machines and gadgets."

"Awesome," I said. Treasure hunting without too much digging sounded a big improvement to me – and my blisters thought it was a result, too.

"Tell you what," Frankie said thoughtfully. "He's coming round to ours this afternoon for this do Mum's having. I'll ask him if we can borrow it. If he says yes, we can have a proper treasure-hunting Sleepover. What do you reckon?"

"Yeahhh!" we all cheered. Sleepovers are always, always the best part of the week but they're even better when we've got a bit of a theme going. And in all the hundreds of Sleepovers we must have had by now, we'd never had a treasure-hunting one. Yet!

"So me and Dad can leave the digging for now," I said. "No point in us wasting our energy if the metal detector is going to tell us if there's anything buried down there or not."

"Too right," Dad said, sounding cheerful. "I'll go and put those spades back in the shed."

"How about if we all meet up at mine tomorrow?" Frankie suggested. "Rosie can report back from the library and I can tell you all what my uncle said about the metal detector. Two o'clock sound all right?"

"Two o'clock it is!" we all agreed. I felt excited already. There's nothing like having a new project to get your teeth into, is there? Especially when there might be TREASURE at the end of it!

The rest of Saturday went quickly. Me and Tom, one of my brothers, took Buster out to the common for a long walk and threw his ball and lots of sticks for him to chase and fetch. Tom had his own ideas about the ring.

"I wouldn't get too hung up on this Roman thing," he said. "I know it would be great, but I'd be dead surprised if the ring was as old as that. Two thousand years old... it's still really shiny and I'm sure a Roman ring wouldn't look that good. Our house is Victorian, isn't it? I mean, think about it – the ring could just have belonged to someone who once lived there, couldn't it?"

"Yeah, I suppose," I admitted. "But we were kind of hoping that there would be lots more treasure to find. It wouldn't be as exciting, finding one single ring and nothing else."

"Yeah, course," Tom said, "but you don't know who might have lived in our house a hundred or so years ago. It could have been a highwayman who went out stealing jewellery from rich ladies. There could be a whole load of old brooches and rings and necklaces down there. Or there could have been a... a man who murdered his wife and buried her in the garden, jewellery and all. I'm surprised you haven't found her skull!"

I giggled. "Who else, then?" I asked. Tom was good at making up funny stories.

"It could have been a family where one of the six daughters was so beautiful that every rich gentleman in the country was after her hand in marriage," he started. "Her father got so sick of people turning up at his house, trying to woo his daughter, that he buried all her trinkets in the garden and locked her in the attic so that she could never see the light of day again."

"Oh, that's a sad one," I said. "And anyway, we don't have an attic."

"OK, the cellar," Tom shrugged. "And the girl's eldest sister – who was ugly in comparison, and who no one ever fancied or wanted to marry – was so jealous of her beautiful sister that she went out in the garden one night, dug up all the trinkets that their father had buried and went to sell them at Cuddington market. Only she missed one of the rings – the one you found."

"That's a horrible story," I complained. "What a mean sister, to do something like that."

"Of course, it could have been an old wise woman who lived in our house," Tom continued, throwing Buster's bouncy ball for him to fetch. "One of those women that everyone else in the village went to for advice and magical potions and spells. Maybe she buried the gold ring as part of a spell to cure a broken heart."

"Oh, I hope so!" I said eagerly. "That's a much nicer idea."

"Or put a curse on someone..." Tom added. "Anyway, let's face it, it's probably none of those. It's probably just a little old lady who lost her ring when she was gardening one day. BORING! Hey, you should get on the computer and look up the census records. Then you'll be able to see all the people that ever lived there – you never know, you could find out something interesting!"

"Tom, you're a genius!" I said excitedly. "That is such a cool idea."

Tom grinned. "Just don't forget whose idea it was when you find all the treasure," he said. "I've got my eye on this mountain bike in the Cuddington Bike Shop..."

"It's yours," I told him. "Deal!"

CHAPTER FOUR

I had exciting dreams all night about masked highwaymen burying bags of gold at the bottom of the garden. When I woke up, it took me a few moments to remember that it had only been a dream, and we hadn't found all the treasures I'd been thinking about. Still, there was the gold ring winking at me from my chest of drawers and I was CONVINCED there would be more to come.

After lunch, I jumped on my bike and cycled over to Frankie's. Our village, Little Wearing, is a couple of miles from Cuddington but most of the journey is pretty flat so it's a good ride. Shame Frankie lives right at the top of the hill though! Sometimes I have to get off my bike and push it, but today I was in such a hurry to get there, I pedalled all the way.

Frankie laughed at my red face when she opened the door. "Lyndz! You look like you've just run a marathon!"

"I feel like it," I puffed, wheeling my bike into her porch. "Are the others here yet?"

"Yeah – just arrived," she replied. "Come into the kitchen – you're just in time to see our new toy."

I grinned from ear to ear. "You've got it already?" I said.

"I certainly have," she said. "Wait till you see it!"

To look at Frankie's face, you'd think it was Christmas day. She goes on about how her uncle loves mad gadgets but she is exactly the same. Give her something new and electronic and she'll be your best friend for life!

In the kitchen, the others were all sitting around the kitchen table. Once I'd sat down with them, Frankie pulled a strange-looking contraption out of a cupboard and promptly brandished it in the air. "Ta-daaaa!" she said. "Meet our new treasure-hunting buddy."

The metal detector looked a bit like a silver, space-age micro-Hoover, if you can imagine something like that. It had a long handle and a small, flattish base. Frankie flicked a switch and the machine made a low humming noise. A red light glowed on the base. "Now, watch this," she instructed us importantly.

WHEE-WHEE-WHEEEEEE! As soon as Frankie ran the metal detector over the cooker, the red light turned green and the low hum became a high-pitched ringing sound.

"Metal hob, you see, on the cooker," Frankie explained. She went over to the sink. WHEE-WHEE-WHEEEEE! "Metal taps!" She went over to the back door. WHEE-WHEE-WHEEEEE! "Metal hinges, keys, lock, bolt!"

Then Frankie came over to us. "Now, anybody got any jewellery on?" she asked. "Don't tell me! Let the metal detector tell me."

She put the detector near Fliss. WHEE-WHEE-WHEEEE! "Easy one," Frankie grinned. "Don't think I've ever SEEN Fliss without her rings and bracelets and earrings!"

Then she moved the detector nearer me. "Is Lyndz wearing any jewellery?" she asked. The light stayed red and the machine just hummed. "No, I don't think so," Frankie said.

"Correct!" I laughed. I'm the sort of person who has jewellery for about ten seconds and then manages to lose it or break it.

"Let's try Rosie," Frankie said and ran the detector around her.

WHEE-WHEE-WHEEEEE!

"Earrings," Rosie said, pushing her earlobes forward to show us her little gold studs. "It's very sensitive, isn't it?"

"It's brilliant," Frankie said happily. "I wish I could keep it! Now, for Kenz. I happen to know that Miss McKenzie isn't a big fan of jewellery so it's hardly worth me doing her, but..."

WHEE-WHEE-WHEEEEEE!

Frankie looked gobsmacked to see the green light flashing as she brought the metal detector nearer Kenny. Kenny grinned and said nothing.

"What have you got on, then, Kenz?" Frankie asked. "You haven't got your ears pierced, I know that..."

"How come? Too chicken?" Fliss teased, poking her tongue out.

"Yeah, you got me," Kenny said sarcastically. "If only I could be as brave as you, Fliss!"

"I'm pretty sure you won't be wearing a necklace, I can see you aren't wearing a ring..." Frankie broke off, frowning. "So what is it?"

Kenny patted her tummy and winked at us. "Finally got it done, didn't I?" she said, sounding smug. "Got my bellybutton pierced yesterday."

"You didn't!" Fliss gasped, her mouth hanging open in shock. "What, and your mum let you?"

"Did it hurt?" I asked. "Did you cry?"

"Of *course* I didn't CRY!" Kenny snorted. "Who do you think I am? Emily Berryman?"

"Let's see it, then," Rosie said. I could tell

she didn't know whether to believe Kenny or not.

"Well, you can't actually see it at the moment because there's a socking great plaster over it," Kenny said, taking a sip of Coke. "But if you don't believe me, why don't you run the metal detector over my tummy for proof?"

Frankie narrowed her eyes, as if she didn't quite trust Kenny, but took the metal detector and held it just above Kenny's belly.

WHEE-WHEE-WHEEEEEE!

"See?" Kenny said. "I told you!"

"Show us the plaster, then," Rosie ordered.

Kenny looked all wide-eyed and innocent. "Rosie Maria Cartwright, I hope you're not saying that you don't believe me!" she said sorrowfully. She stood up and undid the top button of her jeans. Then she started pulling up her T-shirt. "Here you are... OW! OW! Oh!" and she dropped to the floor, clutching her belly and rolling in agony.

"What happened?" I said, rushing round to her side.

"I caught the plaster on my jeans – I must have pulled the ring out – I'm bleeding!" Kenny yelped.

"Quick! Get some ice!" I cried anxiously.

"I'm going to be sick – I don't want to see any blood!" Fliss wailed, turning away.

Frankie put down the metal detector and marched over to her best friend. "Kenny McKenzie, get up right NOW!" she ordered. "Nobody believes a word of it!"

Kenny lay on the floor and burst out giggling. "Lyndz and Fliss did!" she snorted, through her giggles. "Of COURSE I haven't got my bellybutton pierced, you 'nanas – Mum and Dad would hit the roof!" she sniggered, rolling around. She pulled a purse out of her jeans pocket and shook it so that the coins jingled. "It was my money that was setting off the metal detector!"

What did I tell you about Kenny and her wind-ups? Honestly, she just can't resist. Once we'd got over our giggles, we all had a go with the metal detector round the kitchen. It was really cool. I could see why Frankie was so pleased to get her hands on it. We could find a whole load of treasures with it!

In the end, Frankie's mum came down and begged us to stop it for a while because she'd just put baby Izzy down for a nap and really REALLY didn't want us to wake her up. Frankie pulled a face and switched it off. "Izzy spoils all our fun," she grumbled.

"How about I show you what I found yesterday instead?" Rosie said, putting a bag of papers on the table. "This might help us decide where to look for Roman treasures."

"Roman treasures? Do you mean...?" I began, my eyes lighting up.

"I DO mean!" Rosie laughed. "Here, look, I photocopied these old maps." She spread some papers out in front of us and jabbed her finger at a pencil dot on the paper. "Now, believe it or not, this is Cuddington two thousand years ago."

Frankie craned her neck to peer at the dot. "But there's nothing there!"

Rosie nodded. "Yes, exactly," she said. "DERR! Don't you remember our carnival to celebrate Cuddington being one hundred years old?"

"Oh, yeah," Frankie said, looking embarrassed.

"Right, so that's where Cuddington WOULD have been if it had existed," Kenny said.

"Correct," Rosie replied. "Now see these red triangles I've marked? This one is about three miles north of Cuddington, and this one is about two miles south. And that's where there were Roman settlements!"

"No way!" Frankie said excitedly. "Really?"

"Really," Rosie nodded, grinning at all of us. "Most definitely really. And if you think about how many people would have gone between the two settlements – traders and soldiers and..."

"The postman," Fliss put in helpfully.

"Well, yeah, I'm sure people would need to deliver messages too – anyway, LOADS of people must have travelled from one settlement to the other, so it's quite possible that someone could have dropped a gold ring on the way," Rosie said. "Don't you reckon?"

"Wow," Kenny said, looking at the map in fascination. "Let's hear it for Sherlock Cartwright over here!"

"Yeah, nice work," I echoed. "So our ring really could be two thousand years old... I can't believe it."

"Wait, that's not all," Rosie said, pulling out another piece of paper. "One of the librarians helped me do this bit. She showed me how to trace the old map on to a new map – like this. So now we can see exactly where the old settlements were. Look."

We all hunched over the paper. "So the northern one is near where Pickering village is now..." Frankie said, tracing it with her finger.

"...And the southern one is smack bang in the middle of a dual carriageway!" laughed Kenny.

"So we can't really go digging that one up, then," I joked.

"Not really," Rosie said. "I did ask the librarian about Pickering, though. She said there have already been quite a few digs there but they've never found much."

"Until the Sleepover Club came along with their metal detector that is!" whooped Frankie, waving it in the air.

Rosie shook her head sadly. "Er... that's the problem," she said. "It's all fenced off – you can't just go and start digging away. You have to apply for special permission from the council, the librarian said. And that could take WEEKS."

"And like they'd let us go and dig there anyway," Kenny said gloomily. "The Sleepover Club and their pink plastic beach spades!"

We sat in silence for a few moments and then Rosie took out one last piece of paper with a straight yellow line drawn on it. "But there is THIS," she said. "And I think it's the most coo-el thing of all. This is another copy of the Cuddington map with the settlements marked on it. And this line connects the settlements as the most direct route for the Romans."

Fliss shrugged. "Yeah, so?" she asked. "Are we meant to be excited about that line?"

Rosie grinned. "Abso-definitely-lutely," she

said. "Especially when you see where the line goes." She pointed dramatically at the map. "It goes right through your village, Lyndz – see? AND it goes through Cuddington Park – so that's another place we can go looking for Roman treasure!"

CHAPTER FIVE

There were gasps all round when Rosie told us that. Talk about PROOF!

"I can't believe Roman soldiers might have walked through our village," I said. "Wait till I tell my dad."

"Well, it was only fields back then, remember, there wasn't an actual village," Rosie reminded me.

"Yeah, I know but..." I couldn't quite take it in. It's a bit mad to think about people wandering around the place you live two THOUSAND years ago!

"That is soooo cool," Kenny said, her

eyes full of excitement.

"If only we had a time machine!" Frankie said longingly. "We could go back and see how everything looked in Roman times."

"Mrs Pickernose would probably still be around," Fliss said, meaning one of the grumpy old dinner ladies at school. "She must be getting on for about two thousand years old by now!"

"Yeah, and our neighbours," Kenny agreed. "I reckon they were around with the dinosaurs they're so ancient!"

"Look – what are we waiting for?" Frankie said, jumping up suddenly. "Come on – why don't we take the metal detector to Cuddington Park NOW to see if we can find anything interesting? It's on Rosie's line, isn't it? Why don't we go and start checking it out?"

"Definitely," I agreed. After all Rosie's hard work, it would be almost RUDE not to start investigating immediately!

Everyone else felt the same, so, minutes later, we were all on our bikes and away, feeling mega excited about this new development. Frankie had wrapped up the metal detector carefully with the detecting end in a sports bag, which she then tied around herself. It meant she had to cycle quite carefully to stop it banging around too much behind her, but Frankie's house is only a few minutes away from the park, so at least we didn't have too far to go.

Once we were at the park and had chained our bikes to the main railings, Frankie switched the metal detector on and swung it over the grass and path as we walked along. HMMMMMMMM, it went, sounding very thoughtful.

We walked towards the duck pond. HMMMMMMM.

We walked past the duck pond and along the nature trail. HMMMMM.

We walked to the end of the nature trail and towards the playground. WHEE-WHEE-WHEEEEE!

All of us had grown so used to the low humming noise from the metal detector that the shrill ringing almost made us jump out of our skins.

"Wow!" Kenny said. "It certainly lets you know when it's picked something up, doesn't it?"

"We didn't bring any spades!" Frankie wailed suddenly. "I can't believe we didn't bring spades with us. How are we going to dig up the treasure?"

"Er... I don't think we need spades, actually, this time," sharp-eyed Rosie said dryly and pointed to the path. "I reckon that's our 'treasure' right there."

I went over for a closer look – only to see a piece of rusty old broken bike chain at the side of the path. "Oh, great," I groaned. "Is that really it?"

"I reckon," Rosie said, and sure enough, when Frankie ran the detector near it again, the ringing started up. WHEE-WHEE-WHEEEEE!

Kenny kicked the chain away into the undergrowth. "Try again," she said. "We want to be sure, don't we? There still might be something else down there that's setting it off."

But when Frankie passed the detector

over the place where the chain had been seconds before, there was nothing. Not a sausage. Oh, except for HMMMMMMM, of course, but that didn't count.

"Curses," growled Frankie. "Stoopid old bike chain!"

I shrugged. "It was bound to happen ONCE, I suppose," I said. "Next time, it'll be the real thing."

Calm, confident words from yours truly but of course, seconds later, I was proved wrong.

WHEE-WHEE-WHEEEEEE!

"Ooh, that was quick," Fliss said. "What now – the rest of the rusty old bike?"

"No, the handle for the drains manhole, I reckon," Kenny said, kicking it impatiently. "And I don't know about you lot, but I don't fancy going down THERE to look for any treasure!"

"Ugh, no thanks," Fliss said at once, wrinkling up her nose. "Nobody wants to, do they? Because there's no way that I..."

"Fliss, chill," Kenny ordered. "Stop getting your knickers in a twist – none of us is planning to go down into the sewers, treasure or no treasure!"

This happened a few more times. So far the metal detector had told us about a rusty bike chain, a manhole cover, a muddy two pence piece and an umbrella handle. "We're really going to make our fortune with our finds today," Rosie joked as we started walking towards the bowling green.

"Forget Treasure Team – we're more like Trash Team," Frankie said gloomily. "I wish it was a bit more selective – a 'treasure detector' rather than just 'any old rubbish detector'."

"There must be some proper treasure SOMEWHERE," I said, trying to sound positive.

"Yeah, maybe we'll find the rest of the umbrella," Kenny said sarcastically. "That might be worth 20p at a car boot sale if we can mend it!"

"Don't forget our two pence," Rosie added. "If we invest that in a high-interest bank account, we might have made another penny in interest by the time we're all old enough to leave school!"

Fliss frowned. "Well, that's not going to pay for the new shoes I want to buy," she sniffed. "Hey, Frankie, can I have a go with the detector now? Maybe you're not doing it properly."

Frankie's eyebrows shot up into her fringe. "Not doing it properly?" she echoed in disbelief. "I'm doing the best I can, thank you very much!" She thrust the detector at Fliss, looking cross. "Here, if you think you can do any better, you're welcome to it!"

HMMMMMMMM went the detector all the way up to the bowling green, despite Fliss swinging it around over every single blade of grass she could see.

"Not as easy as you think, is it, Fliss?" Frankie said, with a note of triumph creeping into her voice. "And at least I..."

WHEE-WHEE-WHEEEEEE!

Frankie stopped at once as the detector began its loud ringing sound again. We were on the bowling green now and it was Fliss's turn to look triumphant. "See? It was probably the way you were holding it, Frankie," she said smugly.

Frankie's eyes nearly popped out of her head in disbelief. "What do you mean, the way I was holding it?" she said. "You cheeky..." She shook her head and harrumphed loudly. "Anyway, we don't know what set it off yet. Probably nothing – as usual."

"Probably a 1p coin this time," Kenny joked, getting down on her hands and knees and peering at the grass.

It was very strange. We looked and looked but couldn't see anything at all that might have set the metal detector off. And the grass on the bowling green was clipped so short and neat that if there HAD been anything there, it would have been impossible for us to miss it.

"Well, either the metal detector has found a needle or pin that's too tiny for us to see," Rosie said, "or there's something buried there that's setting it off. Check it again, Fliss, will you?"

WHEE-WHEE-WHEEEEEE!

Fliss couldn't wipe the grin off her face. "Oh, my goodness, we really have found buried treasure," she said. "If only we could find out what's down there!"

"Well, what's stopping us?" Kenny wanted to know. Her whole face was lit up with excitement.

Fliss rolled her eyes. "Er... DERRRR! We are in the middle of Cuddington bowling green, and it's broad daylight! We can't just start digging up the green, can we?"

"Why not?" Frankie argued. "There's hardly anyone around to see us. Groundsmen don't work on Sundays, do they? No one will mind if we just have a quick look."

I was with Fliss on this one. "No, Frankie!" I said, feeling a bit shocked at what she and Kenny were suggesting. "We could get in loads of trouble. And we might wreck the bowling green if we dig it up. It's meant to be dead flat, isn't it, like a snooker table? It'll ruin it if we dig great big holes in it."

"Yeah, but we won't dig great BIG holes, just..." Kenny started, but Rosie interrupted.

"We don't have any spades with us, remember?" she pointed out. "Fliss is right –

it's broad daylight and we're going to look soooo obviously like we're up to something if we start scrabbling around, trying to dig up the green with our bare hands."

"So what do we do, then, brainbox?" Frankie asked, sounding a bit peeved. When Rosie starts pointing things out to you in her matter-of-fact way, it's hard to argue with her. She's one of those people who tend to be right most of the time – even if you don't want her to be right!

"I'm not saying we SHOULDN'T dig up the bowling green," Rosie said with a grin. "I'm as keen as you, Frankie, to see what's down there. I'm just saying we need to pick our moment. Be subtle about it."

"You're right – the Sleepover Club can do 'subtle'. If people see us digging for treasure, they'll all want a piece of it," Kenny said. "We've got to do it when no one else is around."

"What – like the middle of the night?" Fliss asked, looking concerned. "'Cos there's no WAY my mum is going to let me go out after dark. Anything could happen, you know. And anyway, this park would be well creepy in the dark. There might be bats or ANYTHING flapping around and..."

"Keep your hair on, Fliss," Rosie sighed. "No one said anything about coming to the park in the middle of the night, did they? My mum would have a fit about us doing that too – everybody's mum would. No, I was thinking more about creeping out first thing in the morning when it's just light and no one else is around."

"Cool idea!" said Kenny. "We could do it after our next Sleepover – set our alarms for dead early the morning after and go off on our bikes. That way we can have a good look under the green before the groundsman starts work."

"We could have the Sleepover at mine," Frankie suggested at once. "My house is nearest the park, isn't it?"

"We could have a ROMAN Sleepover," I said, getting into the swing of it. "We could wear togas and be gladiators and stuff!"

"Did the Romans eat mashed potato, by any chance?" Fliss wanted to know.

Rosie giggled. "I think they ate really weird things like roast dormice, didn't they? Do you think your mum will have a recipe, Frankie?"

"A Roman Sleepover is a wicked idea," Frankie said, looking pleased. "Oh, I can hardly wait a whole week to come back and do some digging here, though – it seems ages away. How are we going to get through it, when we know there could be a whole stash of buried treasure, right here, under our noses, in Cuddington Park?"

CHAPTER SIX

Everyone's faces fell when Frankie said that. She was right. The week was going to go soooo slowly. It was going to be absolutely unbearable. Knowing you might have found treasure but not being able to get to it – talk about torture!

"We could just have a quick scrabble at the soil with our fingers," impatient Kenny said. "No one will notice us, I bet. Just a little, little, teeny tiny peek..." As our all-action girl, Kenny was going to find it harder than anyone to wait out the week.

"No, Kenny," Fliss told her sternly.

"Imagine – if we got caught, we could be in the *Cuddington Post* and everything for vandalising the park. My mum would just KILL me, and my gran would be sooo disappointed." She shook her head, looking serious. "And I'd never be allowed out for another Sleepover with you again. I'd have to leave the Sleepover Club and everything – and then I'd NEVER get my shopping trip."

"Glad we mean so much to you," Frankie muttered.

"A teeny tiny scrabble isn't going to show us much anyway," Rosie said reasonably. "Roman stuff is going to be buried way deeper than that, isn't it? We're going to need spades to do it properly."

"She's right – and so is Fliss," I said. "Let's wait till next Saturday morning to see what the metal detector has found. We can always go back to my garden now to see if there's anything else there."

Kenny's face brightened. "Cool idea, Lyndz," she said with a smile. "I'd forgotten about that. Not one but TWO places to look for treasure – how lucky are we?"

Everyone was cheered up by my idea. "Let's just have one last sweep over the green with the metal detector to hear that ringing sound again," said Frankie. "It's just such a great noise!"

WHEE-WHEE-WHEEEEEE!

We all stared at each other in shocked excitement as the detector went off just about everywhere we took it on the bowling green.

"There must be treasure absolutely all over the place," Fliss said with a grin. "We are going to find such a lot of stuff next Saturday if this detector is telling us even half the truth!"

From all the ringing sounds, it did seem to be suggesting there was a LOT of treasure down there, not just one measly little piece! Suddenly, Saturday seemed even FURTHER away than it had five minutes ago. I was just about to give in to temptation and start tearing up the grass with my bare hands when I saw two old couples coming on to the green with their bowling bags, ready to play a game.

"Uh oh, oldies alert," Kenny hissed. "Time to make tracks!"

We got on our bikes again before they could ask us what we'd been doing – you don't half get some nosy people around Cuddington who try to stop you doing anything remotely interesting – and cycled over towards my house. All of us were feeling like we were really on to something BIG now.

"I know we've done loads and loads of great things together as the Sleepover Club," Frankie said as we rode along Cuddington Park Road, "but this does feel like a really REALLY exciting one, don't you think?"

"Too right," I agreed. "I just know we're going to find something totally awesome in the park."

"The way the metal detector was just going mad everywhere we went on the bowling green – I mean, there must be loads of stuff down there," Rosie said, beaming broadly. "And it's the sort of place that no one would even dream of looking. No one except the Sleepover Club, that is," she added proudly.

"Yay for the Sleepover Club!" Kenny shouted, taking both hands off the handlebars and clapping them over her head. "We rule at treasure hunting!"

"We rooooooole the schoooool!" we all chorused back at her. (If you didn't know, that's a quote from the film *Grease* which we've all seen about a trillion times.)

"Now all we need to do is dig up a whole treasure chest in Lyndz's garden to keep us going until Saturday," joked Frankie. "That's the only thing that will stop me going mad with impatience."

"Yeah – just think if we did find TWO lots of treasure," Fliss said dreamily. "Can you imagine how gutted everyone at school would be? Their faces!"

"Hey, I forgot to say – my brother Tom was coming out with all these ideas about the ring, you know," I told them as we started cycling into my village. "He said he didn't think it looked old enough to be Roman – but said it could have been buried by a highwayman a hundred years ago – or maybe by a witch who'd used it in a spell to cure a broken heart!"

"Witches, schmitches," Rosie scoffed. "Do you really believe in all that rubbish?"

"Well, maybe the highwayman, then," I said. "Like Dick Turpin! Imagine – he could have robbed all the rich people in the village and come to bury the loot in OUR garden. There could be all sorts of goodies down there."

"Cool!" Frankie beamed.

"Who's Dick Turnip?" Fliss wanted to know.

"Dick TURNIP!" Kenny snorted. "He was this Swede-ish guy – boom, boom!"

"Oh, Fliss, don't you know anything?" Rosie groaned. "He was a famous highwayman who would hold up carriages at night time with a pistol or sword or something. He wore a mask over his eyes and this big cloak, and he used to shout, 'Your money or your life!' And everyone was so scared of him that they handed over all their money and jewellery."

"What, so he was a thief?" Fliss asked, sounding horrified. "Well, that's not very nice, is it? I don't know if I want to find anything belonging to him, thank you very much!"

The rest of us rolled our eyes at each other. What was Fliss LIKE?!

It was funny how we'd started talking about thieves, though, because that's all Mum could talk about when we got back home. As we leaned our bikes against the front wall and went inside, she practically pounced on us.

"I want you all to be aware," she said as she poured us all glasses of lemonade, "there's a thief in the village. You'd better bring your bikes round the back, girls, just in case. Alice next door was telling me all about it. Mrs Brody from number 25 has had her silver bracelet stolen, and Lisa Jones from over the road had a ring taken."

I was nearly as shocked as Mum. Little Wearing is only a small village and I've always felt really safe here. Everyone knows everyone else, and people look out for each other. I couldn't believe someone was going around stealing stuff. Nothing bad EVER happens here.

"What, so were their houses broken into?" Kenny asked with interest. After being a doctor or a vet, Kenny really fancies being a detective when she's older. I could tell she was taking the opportunity to get some practice in early.

Mum handed the lemonade round. "Well, that's the funny thing," she said. "The jewellery was taken almost from under their noses. Mrs Brody left her bracelet on a back windowsill while she was weeding the garden. She can't think how anyone could have gone through her garden to steal it without her noticing them."

"What about Lisa?" I asked. Lisa Jones lives over the road and is the same age as my brother Stuart. She's really pretty and friendly, and goes riding at the same stables as me. I couldn't imagine why anyone would want to steal anything from her.

"Similar thing," Mum said. "She was washing her dad's car for him and left her ring and watch on the front wall. The strange thing is that her ring was taken but her watch wasn't – and it was a good one, too.

She can't understand why the thief left it and just took the ring."

"I bet the ring blew off the wall," Rosie said. "Or maybe she wasn't even wearing it in the first place – just thought she had been. It's probably somewhere in her bedroom."

Mum shook her head. "No, she wears that ring all the time apparently. It was a present from her grandmother for her sixteenth birthday, and she knows she was wearing it on that day."

"Weird," said Kenny. "Must be a very sneaky thief to get away without being noticed like that. Sounds like a cat burglar to me."

Fliss looked at her as if she was mad. "Why would a cat want to steal a bracelet and a ring?" she laughed. "Quick, Lyndz – better check what your cats have been doing all day – see if they've stashed a load of stolen jewellery somewhere!" Then she started laughing even harder. "Hey, I've just had a thought. What if... what if that ring we found in your garden was put there by the cats?"

The rest of us all groaned. "FLISS!" Frankie said, trying not to corpse herself laughing. "A cat burglar isn't a real CAT who steals things – it's just a type of burglar who's ultra-sneaky. You know, cat-like."

Fliss stopped laughing abruptly. "I knew that," she said, going red. "I was just..."

"Yeah, yeah," I said, giggling at her. "Whatever. Shall we go out into the garden now and start treasure hunting?"

"Yeah, let's see if your moggies have hidden anything else out there," Kenny teased. "Honestly – you have to watch out for these cat burglars, you know. Outrageous!"

This time Frankie wasn't letting Fliss anywhere near the metal detector after her cheeky comments in the park. Fliss had found the bowling green treasure and there was no way Frankie wanted anyone else to steal her thunder. She reckoned that as *she'd* got the metal detector in the first place, it was only fair that she should be the one to find any treasure with it.

We wheeled our bikes around the back and then started on the real work. "Right, let's try these flowerbeds first, then," Frankie said, switching the detector on, and waving it over the flowers that were nearest. HMMMMM, it went.

Then we tried the lawn, up and down in straight lines as if we were mowing it, just to make sure we covered every little centimetre. HMMMMMMM.

"How about under the tree again where we found the ring in the first place?" I asked.

"DERRR! The most obvious place in the whole garden and we didn't think of it sooner!" Kenny groaned. "I was too busy wondering about the thief."

We took the metal detector right to the far end of the garden where the ash tree was. "This one," I said, pointing it out to Frankie.

As soon as Frankie stepped under the tree with the detector, we immediately heard our new favourite noise. WHEE-WHEE-WHEEEEE!

"Yay!" Fliss cheered. "Let's get digging!"

"Hang on – what's that?" Kenny asked, getting on her knees and picking something out of the grass. She held it up – it was a tarnished old necklace.

"Well, that doesn't look very Roman," Rosie said at once. "Is it yours, Lyndz?"

I shook my head. "Nope," I said. "Nor Mum's. She doesn't wear necklaces – they make her feel itchy."

"It's weird that it was just on the ground, not buried or anything," Frankie frowned. "Where did it come from?"

"Maybe the thief dropped it!" Fliss squeaked excitedly. "Maybe he was sneaking through your garden, Lyndz, and dropped it under the tree!"

Kenny screwed up her face. "Why would anyone want to steal this, though?" she asked, holding her palm out so we could all see the necklace. "I mean – it looks really cheap and tacky and old. Why steal this and leave Lisa's watch?"

I put the necklace in my pocket. "Let's keep looking," I said. "I'll ask Mum about this later – see if she knows whose it is."

It was really disappointing. After all the excitement of the gold ring and the buried treasure under the bowling green, there didn't seem to be anything else in the garden, even though we spent ages running the metal detector over every leaf, flower and blade of grass.

We all felt a bit flat when Frankie finally admitted defeat and switched off the metal detector.

"I hate not knowing stuff," Kenny grumbled. "I hate not knowing what's under the bowling green, I hate not knowing where that gold ring came from and I hate not knowing whose necklace that is!"

"And who the thief is," I added, fingering the necklace in my pocket. "There are just too many mysteries around at the moment."

"Cheer up," Frankie said, wrapping up the metal detector again and strapping it to herself. "At least we've got Saturday to look forward to. And I'll make sure Friday night's Sleepover is a real Roman stonker, too, to get us in the mood!"

After they'd all gone home, I locked up my bike carefully in the shed. There was no way I wanted to get that stolen – especially not when I was going to need it for our dawn raid on the bowling green next week!

CHAPTER SEVEN

Just as we'd thought, the week dragged by as slow as anything. At school, Mrs Weaver kept giving us surprise spelling tests to keep us on our toes, as she put it – although we all reckoned it was out of sheer meanness. "She probably can't think of anything else to teach us," Kenny muttered darkly as, for the third day on the trot, more of the dreaded test papers were passed around.

I didn't get any further with trying to solve the necklace mystery either – I drew a complete blank with Mum and didn't know who else I could ask about it. The only good bit of news was that the thief seemed to have gone quiet as nobody else had anything stolen in the village. But as to who the thief was in the first place – well, that was another unsolved mystery that was bugging me to death!

There was definitely an enormous Sleepover Club sigh of relief when it came to Friday afternoon and Mrs Weaver said it was time to go home.

"Thank GOODNESS," Fliss said, with great feeling. "I just couldn't STAND any more tests or sitting still or trying not to think about treasure hunting for another second."

"I know," Kenny said, grabbing her coat off the peg and making a run for the door. "This week has just about driven me bonkers!"

We all felt the same. Not even the M&Ms, our two biggest enemies, 'accidentally' tripping me and Rosie up outside the school gates could wipe the smiles off our faces.

"Is that the best you can do?" Rosie said sweetly, brushing the dust off her skirt. "You'll have to try a bit harder if you want to upset us, you know."

"Yeah, you just wait until Monday," I added with a smirk. "You're going to be soooo gutted when you find out what we've been up to."

THAT took the smirks off their faces, I can tell you.

"What are you on about now, Collins?" Emily sneered. "Living in airy-fairy land, are we?" She was trying to look like she didn't care but I could tell she was really dying to know what we had got planned.

Kenny winked solemnly at them. "Top secret, I'm afraid. We could tell you – but then we'd have to kill you," she said, then looked thoughtful. "Hey, that wouldn't be so bad though, would it? Come on, Frankie, we'll get Emily, the rest of you get Emma!" She was only joking, but as she made a dart towards Emily, both M&Ms screamed and started running down the road away from us.

All five of us burst out laughing at their frightened faces. "Diddums! Quick – get back home to Mummy!" Kenny bawled after them.

Ahhh... it's always nice to have a little M&M moment to start off the weekend!

"I love winding those two up," Kenny giggled contentedly, passing round a bag of jelly babies. "They are just so dumb; they'll fall for anything you tell them."

"It's going to drive them mad, wondering what we're up to this weekend as well," Frankie said, biting a jelly baby's head off with relish. "It's always good to make them suffer a bit!"

Frankie's house is quite close to the school so we walked back, swinging our Sleepover bags excitedly. There's nothing like that Friday feeling, is there? Especially when you've got a full-on Sleepover and some serious treasure hunting ahead of you!

We'd been quizzing Frankie all week about what she had planned for the Roman Sleepover but she'd been very mysterious and just kept tapping her nose annoyingly. "My gran says, 'All good things come to he who waits'," was all she'd say. "And 'she' who waits gets even better things!"

"Stop talking in riddles and just tell us," moaned Kenny in despair, but Frankie wouldn't budge. It wasn't until we got back to her house that Friday afternoon that she finally let us in on her plans.

"First things first," she said, leading us through to the kitchen. "We've got to look the part!"

There was a huge heap of old white bed sheets on her kitchen table plus a small pile of leaves on a side plate.

"Is this what I think it is?" Rosie smiled.

"Yep – togas!" Frankie replied, handing us each a sheet. "Don't gawp like that, Fliss! You know what a toga is, don't you?"

"Well, yes, kind of," Fliss said hesitantly. In other words – no!

"All the Romans wore them," Kenny said, draping her sheet around her shoulders. "You just sort of wrap it around yourself like this... Er, no... that's not right. Maybe it's like this..."

"Hang on, hang on," Frankie said. "I thought we'd customise them a bit first. I've got some of that fabric paint that puffs up when you warm it with a hair dryer, and some glitter pens and other stuff. I reckon wearing togas all night might be a bit boring unless we brighten them up a bit. Agree?"

"Agree!" we all chorused, sitting down around the table.

I pointed at the plate of leaves. "And these are for...?" I prompted.

"Oh, yes!" Frankie said. "Well, as well as togas, the Romans used to wear sort of crown things made of laurel leaves on their heads. But these ones are just leaves I found in the garden, because I didn't know anyone who had a laurel tree." She looked a bit apologetic. "And I couldn't find enough for a whole crown each so we're just going to have to make do with a few each. We can fix them in our hair with hair clips."

"Cool!" Rosie said, passing paintbrushes around to everyone. "You've thought of everything, Frankie." Then she giggled. "Hey, didn't the Romans wear those great big leather sandals? And when it got too cold, they wore *socks* and sandals. *We* don't have to wear them as well, do we?"

"Nooo, not socks and sandals!" Fliss yelped. "That's, like, soooo unfashionable, you know." She was looking majorly alarmed at the thought.

"I thought we could just have bare feet," Frankie said, sprinkling a load of blue glitter on to her sheet. "All right, Fliss?"

Fliss smiled with relief. "Fine by me," she said. "What is everyone putting on their toga, then? I can't think what to do on mine."

"I'm putting my name and doing the Leicester City badge so it looks like a football toga," Kenny said. (In case you didn't know, she's a complete sports freak and loves her footy.)

"I'm doing some red and white roses for my name," Rosie said, dabbing away with a paintbrush. "Only you'll have to take my word for it, 'cos they look more like red and white polka dots so far."

"I'm drawing a horse," I said, and the others all groaned.

"Surprise, surprise!" Frankie said. "Pet Rescue Collins goes for the animal option!"

I stuck my tongue out at her and grinned. I draw horses all the time because I absolutely love them more than anything. I'm still rubbish at drawing them, though. I can never quite get the neck right. "Hey, the

Romans used to ride around on horseback so there!" I said, doing little strokes of paint for the mane.

"Yeah, yeah," Frankie said. "Well, I'm just doing some glittery swirls and some Roman numerals. I can't think of anything else to do."

Fliss giggled. "I'm going to paint a pair of trendy shoes on mine, then, just to show that I'm definitely NOT a sandal-wearing kind of Roman girl!"

Once our paintings and glued bits were dry, Frankie's mum helped us put our togas on and safety-pinned them at the shoulder to keep them in place. Then we all clipped some leaves into our hair like mini crowns.

When we'd finished laughing our heads off at how stoooopid we looked, Frankie got us playing a Roman version of Fizz Buzz while her mum started making tea.

It was really difficult. Do you know how to play Fizz Buzz? Mrs Weaver taught us at school and it's meant to help you learn your times tables, but if you're rubbish at maths (like me and Fliss) it's not much fun at all.

Basically, you take it in turns to say one number each, getting higher in order – like one, two, three. But for every number that can be divided by three, you have to say Fizz instead. And for every number that can be divided by four, you say Buzz. And for every number you can divide by five, you say Quack. And, just to make it even more complicated, for numbers like twelve that can be divided by three and four, you have to say Fizz Buzz.

I know, I know. Sounds more like hard work than fun to me, too. Frankie is brilliant at maths, though, so she likes it, and she got us playing this Roman version she'd made up where, instead of saying "One, Two, Fizz, Buzz" etc, you had to say the numbers as ROMAN numerals. Do you know what they are? They're the ones that go: I, II, III, IV, V, VI and all that. So one would be 'eye' and two would be 'eye eye'. Talk about confusing!

Luckily, everyone else found it a bit hard-going as well (apart from Maths-head Frankie) and then Frankie and Kenny got into an argument about what the Roman numeral for twenty was so that stopped the game. Phew-ee. Even more luckily, just then, Frankie's mum shouted that tea was ready so that was the end of that!

"What on earth have you got planned for tea?" Rosie asked as we walked into the kitchen. "You WERE only joking about the roast dormice, weren't you?"

"There's no way I'm eating a cute little mouse!" I said at once.

"Nor me," Fliss agreed with a shudder.

"Oh," said Frankie. "I told Mum we wanted it to be truly authentic."

"Spaceman, you didn't." Fliss clutched at me in alarm as, there on the table, was a plate of pastry-covered mice – their little tails poking out.

"Ugh, gross," said Rosie, going green.

Just then Kenny picked up one of the dormice and gave it a sniff.

"Kenny, noooo!" we all shouted.

"You twits!" she said, waggling her eyebrows at us. "I smell veggie sausage rolls with string tails!"

"We so knew that," the rest of us chorused with relief, as Frankie collapsed with laughter.

"Sorry, girls, nothing as exciting as roast dormice," Frankie's mum smiled, doling out steaming scoops of pasta on to our plates. "The best I could come up with was Italian food. When in Rome and all that..."

"YUM!" Pizza and pasta and garlic bread... my favourite.

The rest of the Sleepover was a bit more fun than Frankie's awful game. We watched Frankie's mum's *Gladiator* video after promising to close our eyes at the gory bits and then, once we were ready for bed, had a few rounds of International Gladiators ourselves, taking it in turns to be Maximus and the tigers. I haven't giggled so much in ages at the sight of Kenny in her pyjamas and leaf hair clips wrestling with Frankie and Fliss, and then all three of them falling off the bed in a heap.

When we were all Roman-d out, we lay in our sleeping bags in a line on the floor, and talked sleepily about all the treasure we were going to find the next day.

Frankie switched off her bedside lamp. "Good night, treasure hunters!" she said softly.

"Good night!" we all replied, and fell asleep, just like that.

CHAPTER EIGHT

Frankie had set her alarm for six o'clock and as soon as it went off, I felt wide awake and dead excited. It's funny how I usually have to drag myself out of bed at half-past seven for school – but waking up at six to go treasure hunting was no problem!

We got washed and dressed and then crept downstairs quietly to grab some breakfast before we went off on our mission. Frankie had told her parents we were going to go for an early bike ride so that they wouldn't worry when they got up – but she hadn't told them just how early we were going to go. And she certainly hadn't told them that we were planning to dig up Cuddington bowling green in search of treasure!

Frankie handed round some apples and bananas. "Let's not waste time making toast or tea or anything," she said. "Let's just take these with us and get going. I can't wait any longer."

"Agreed," said Kenny and Rosie, stuffing the fruit into their pockets.

"Let's hit the road," I said, as Frankie wrapped up the metal detector.

"Gold and silver and Roman coins, look out," Fliss said, her eyes wide with excitement. "The Sleepover Club is coming to get you!"

It felt like a real adventure, getting on our bikes so early in the morning and pedalling off to the park. The sun was just coming up as we left the house and there was silvery dew still sparkling on people's lawns. It was strange to be up and about so early on a Saturday morning, when most normal people were still snoozing in their beds.

"It's so quiet," I said to the others as we zoomed down Frankie's road. "It's as if we're the only people left in Cuddington!"

Frankie's face brightened. "Hey, did you ever see that cool film about a man who woke up to find he was the only person left alive in the world?" she said. "Just imagine if that was what was happening to us right now... only the Sleepover Club is left on planet earth and we have to fight off the aliens who have eaten everybody else..."

"They better not have laid a finger on my mum," Fliss said fiercely. "Or Andy. Or Callum. Or..."

"I think Izzy might have survived," Rosie said dryly. "I heard her gurgling over the baby monitor, back at yours, Frankie."

"She won't be much use," Kenny said. "How can a baby fight aliens?"

"Ahhh, she might have special powers," Frankie said, warming to her idea. "Maybe that's how she survived the alien attack in the first place."

"You lot have all gone completely bonkers," I said, giggling so much that my bike started wobbling around in the road. "I don't think you got enough sleep!"

"I'm with Lyndz," Rosie said. "Frankie, I'm starting to think that YOU are an alien, the nonsense you come out with sometimes."

Frankie looked delighted, as if Rosie had paid her the biggest compliment. "In my dreams," she sighed. "Now that WOULD be something to get excited about."

At this point, we reached the park and saw that the gates were padlocked. The sign on the gate said that the park wouldn't be open until seven o'clock.

"It's only six-thirty," Kenny said, checking her watch.

"Excellent – so no one will be around to disturb us," Frankie said cheerfully.

"Er... Frankie, aren't you forgetting something?" Fliss said, frowning. "We can't actually get in ourselves, can we?"

Kenny and Frankie looked at her as if she was mad. "A couple of crummy little gates aren't going to stop us," Kenny said scornfully. "Even baby Izzy could scale those two, I reckon."

"Yeah, they'll have to try a bit harder than that if they want to keep me away from that treasure," Frankie said. "Right – who wants a leg-up?"

Fliss bit her lip. "I'm not sure about this," she said, sounding anxious. "We might get into trouble if we just... go in there."

"Oh, no one will know," Rosie said breezily, padlocking her bike to the railings. "Right, Frankie, here I come."

She put a foot on Frankie's linked hands and hoisted herself on to the top of the gates. Then she jumped down to the other side and grinned. "Easy peasy," she said. "Who's next, then?"

One by one, we all clambered over and dropped to the ground. "I'm not happy about this," Fliss muttered. "If we get caught, then you lot MADE me do this, right?"

I was feeling a bit nervous about it all, too. My mum and dad are quite strict about sticking to rules and I knew they'd be cross if they could see me now, backside in the air, as I heaved myself over the gates.

"Oh, rules are made to be broken," Kenny

said, shrugging off our worries. "Besides, we only need to keep our heads down for half an hour. When it gets to seven o'clock we're allowed to be in the park anyway. Trust me – it's no biggie."

All the same, it did feel weird to be sneaking around the park on our own. I crossed my fingers and hoped we wouldn't get caught. I didn't want to have to talk my way out of this one!

We made our way to the bowling green as quickly and quietly as possible. Once there, we went over to the corner where we'd first heard the metal detector go off. "We won't risk using the metal detector until it's gone seven," Frankie decided. "Far too noisy – we don't want to alert the groundsman that the treasure hunters are a bit on the early side, do we?"

"This was definitely where it was going off anyway," Rosie said. "So unless anyone has been in this week and taken all the treasure before us..."

We looked at the perfect lawn. "Not unless they've magicked it out of the ground without any digging," I said. "This grass hasn't seen a spade for a while, has it?"

"Well, it's about to see five spades right now," Kenny grinned. "Let's get going!"

After waiting all week for this very moment, when it came to plunging a spade into the neatly clipped grass, all of us were a bit on the hesitant side. Suddenly, we felt dead guilty about what we were about to do.

"Er... who's going to go first?" Rosie asked, as we stood there, spades in hand. "Anyone volunteering to be the first to sacrifice the bowling green to the treasure-hunting gods?"

"OK, OK, here goes nothing," Kenny said dramatically and sank her spade into the grass. "There! The first cut is the deepest – or whatever they say. Anyone going to join me?"

Nobody needed asking twice after that. In went the spades and soon the digging was well underway. "No one is going to mind too much when we dig up a whole hoard of Roman treasure anyway," Frankie reasoned. "In fact, they'll be well chuffed, I reckon."

"And we can even treat them to a brand new bowling green with some of the money we make if they kick up a fuss," Rosie added.

"And if they're STILL not happy, then it's 'turf' luck," Kenny giggled, throwing a clod of earth over her shoulder. "Oops! Sorry, Frankie!"

"Kenz, how did you ever get on the netball team with an aim like that?" Frankie moaned, brushing soil off her fleece.

Kenny gave her a wide-eyed look. "Who's saying that I DIDN'T aim at you?" she said sweetly. "Hot shot McKenzie hits the target again!"

"Right, I'll remember that," Frankie grumbled. "Guess who won't be getting second breakfast when we get back to my house?"

Kenny shrugged. "Who cares? I'll be able to buy my own breakfast when we find the treasure – and it'll be a lot better than anything you can make!"

"IF we find any treasure," Rosie said. "It was definitely here, wasn't it, that the metal detector was going off?"

We all agreed that we were digging in the right spot. "Remember what my dad told us," I said. "Roman treasure isn't going to be right under the surface, is it? It's going to be way, way down."

"Yeah, covered with thousands of years' worth of soil," Fliss said, pulling a face at her spade. "It's going to take us FOREVER to get to it!"

Frankie gave her a stern look. "I hope you're not wimping out on us already, Felicity," she said, wagging a finger. "I mean, just say the word if you don't want any of the treasure and you can go home and we'll spend all the money without you..."

Fliss looked alarmed at the thought of losing out on her shopping spree. "No – I wasn't saying that, Frankie," she said quickly. "I just meant... er... it's lucky that we got up so early because it might take us a while to get to the treasure – but it'll be worth it, of course!"

At the thought of several hours' digging ahead of us, we all put our heads down and got stuck in again. The sky was getting lighter and we suddenly saw a jogger on the path at the top of the hill. "Well, it's seven o'clock," Kenny said suddenly, looking at her watch. "So at least we're allowed to be here now."

"Yeah – shame we're not really supposed to be—" CLONK!

Rosie's voice stopped abruptly as her spade hit something hard. Her mouth dropped open and we all froze on the spot, looking at each other. Awesome… This was it! Buried treasure! We'd found it! We crowded around Rosie, trying to peer down at what her spade had struck.

"Now, carefully," Fliss instructed. "Remember what I said about *Time Team*? How they scrape away the soil gently…"

Kenny plunged her hand down into the hole that Rosie had been digging. "It feels like metal," she said, her eyes bright with excitement. "Quick, Rosie, start digging around it. Let's see what we've got!"

Rosie had just picked up her spade to dig a little further, though, when…

"Hey! You girls! What on EARTH do you think you're doing?"

The five of us spun round, half guilty, half annoyed that someone had interrupted us at the crucial moment.

"Uh oh. Rumbled," Kenny said under her breath.

There, coming towards us, were four old men dressed in bowling blazers and carrying bowling bags. All four of them were red in the face with anger. Oh, no. Who would have thought bowls players would be such early risers?!

When they'd reached us, the tallest of the four started shouting. "You hooligans! What do you think you're doing, vandalising the bowling green? Today of all days! Don't you know there's a county bowls tournament on this morning? Look what you've done!"

None of us dared reply. He looked so furious I was worried he was going to have a heart attack on the spot. I looked down at my feet and suddenly realised how much of the bowling green we'd dug up. He was right.

We'd wrecked it. No wonder he thought we were hooligans.

"We're really sorry," Fliss said, looking close to tears. Her bottom lip started wobbling all over the place. "We didn't know there was a tournament on today. Honestly!"

"There are signs up all over the park about the tournament," another of the men started shouting. "Can't you read? Don't they teach you anything in schools these days? Or did you think you'd sabotage it? From the Pickering team, are you, eh?"

"If you must know, we're digging for treasure," Kenny said defiantly. "And we're sorry about your tournament but we've actually just found something underground, so if you don't mind..."

"Treasure?" snorted the tall man. He really was looking as if he was about to explode. "Wait until the groundsman finds out about this. Not to mention the police!" And with that, he dumped his bag and went striding off across the green, in search of the groundsman, no doubt.

The second man who had spoken took out a little notepad. "Right – names and addresses, girls," he said bossily. "I'm sure your parents will be interested in hearing what you've been doing. You first!" he ordered, pointing at me.

"L-L-Lyndsey Collins," I stammered, but Frankie started talking over me.

"No, wait," she said and began explaining about the Roman maps and the metal detector and the ring we'd found in my garden.

One of the men, who hadn't said anything until now, interrupted her. "So the metal detector has been going off all over the bowling lawn, has it, and you think it must be treasure?" he said.

"YES!" we all chorused. Finally, someone who understood!

Or did he? He was looking thin-lipped and shaking his head. "The reason the metal detector went off here," he said slowly, as if we were all complete morons, "is because there are underground heating pipes below the green, that stop it freezing over in the winter. NOT because there is any buried treasure, Roman or otherwise!"

CHAPTER NINE

Fliss burst into tears and, to be honest, I felt like doing the same thing. Underground heating pipes! How could we have been so stupid? Even brave Kenny went quiet and looked at her feet. It wasn't just the guilt of the terrible thing we'd done, it was the disappointment that we weren't going to find any treasure when we'd all been so convinced we would.

The kindest-looking man of the four passed Fliss a handkerchief. "Come on, don't cry," he said. "Anyone can make a mistake. And at least you've only dug up one side of the bowling green. I'm sure we can cordon it off somehow – we won't have to cancel the tournament."

"It'll be highly irregular," the thin-lipped man sniffed. "The Cuddington members WON'T be pleased. And what are the Pickering team going to think?"

Just then the groundsman rolled up with a horrible smirk on his face. "Oh dear, oh dear, oh dear," he said. "Looks like you'll be paying for this out of your pocket money for a long time, girls."

Fliss sobbed even louder at that.

"Oh yes," the groundsman said. "Council policy – vandals who damage council property have to pay for it. Now, let's have your names and addresses. I won't call the police this time but I WILL call your parents. Do they know anything about this?"

We shook our heads miserably. I was feeling sick at the thought of how my parents would react when they heard the slimy groundsman telling them what we'd been up to. He looked as if he couldn't wait to get on the telephone right away and get us all into trouble.

"Right," he said once he'd scribbled all our details down. "I don't want to see any of you five on this bowling green again. Next time, it'll be a matter for the police. Understand?"

"Yes," I said, feeling shaky at the thought.

"Good," he said. "Now take your spades and hop it. Don't let me catch you here again."

"You won't," Kenny muttered under her breath as we all slunk away. "What a creep – look at him, rubbing his hands at the thought of grassing us up. What a lamebrain!"

Nobody said much as we walked back through the park to get our bikes. Our fantastic treasure-hunting weekend had gone horribly, HORRIBLY wrong. Fliss was still sniffling into the handkerchief.

"My mum's going to KILL me," she wailed. "I said we shouldn't have done it, didn't I? Didn't I SAY?"

"All right, all right," Frankie said gloomily. "No need to go on and on about it, Fliss.

We're ALL going to get killed by our mums, OK? Does that make you feel any better?"

The groundsman was obviously the efficient sort because by the time we got back to Frankie's, all it took was the look on Frankie's mum's face when she opened the front door to make us realise that she knew – and that she was hopping mad.

"Girls, I think it's best if you go straight back to your homes," she said in an icy voice. "Francesca – a word in the kitchen, please. Alone."

Frankie's mum is normally so jolly that it was actually quite scary to see her looking so mad. Me, Kenny, Rosie and Fliss crept upstairs and packed our overnight bags as quietly as little mice, and then made our way downstairs again. Frankie came to say goodbye and her eyes looked all bloodshot and puffy. Now, Frankie isn't a softy like me and Fliss – she NEVER cries. So I knew that whatever Frankie's mum had said to her, it must have been truly awful.

"I'm grounded for, like, ever, and I can't phone any of you all weekend," she whispered as we hugged goodbye. "No pocket money for a month either, worst luck. So see you at school on Monday, yeah? And good luck with your parents."

Then her mum appeared with a long list of chores for Frankie to do, so we decided to get going.

"Time to face the music," Kenny groaned, as she swung a leg over her bike. "I've got a feeling this is going to turn out to be a long, hard, horrible weekend, you know."

"Good luck everyone," Rosie said. "See you all on Monday – if we're all still alive, that is."

As I cycled away with my bag over my shoulders, I started to wish that Fliss and I had tried harder to talk the others out of our treasure-digging idea. I should have known it would all go pear-shaped – the Sleepover Club never seem to be able to get things to go to plan. There was a huge knot in my stomach, just thinking about how cross and disappointed Mum and Dad were going to be.

I don't know about you, but it's the disappointment thing that always gets me. I know angry parents aren't exactly a barrel of laughs either but it's when my mum or dad say those awful words – "We're really disappointed in you, Lyndsey." Aaaaargh! It's a killer! Instant guilt attack or what?

Anyway, this time round it was no different. Sure enough, their faces when I got home – Dad shaking his head, looking puzzled and Mum just looking sad – were enough to make me burst into tears. Then the telling off bit came and made me cry even harder. Just like Frankie, I was grounded all weekend with no phone calls allowed, and no pocket money for a month. And also just like Frankie, my mum had a list of jobs for me to do around the house to keep me out of any more trouble, as she put it. I even had to miss my riding lesson. THAT's how bad it was.

I was in the middle of gloomily scrubbing the bath, wondering if my mum and dad would ever forgive me or if I was doomed to be the black sheep of the family from now on, when Tom stuck his head round the door. He had a big grin on his face.

"Lyndz, you berk, what were you thinking of?" he said, rolling his eyes at me. "Don't tell me you were REALLY looking for treasure under the bowling green, were you? Seriously?"

I nodded sulkily. The last thing I wanted was Tom to start teasing me about our treasure hunt when I was feeling so fed up. "Yeah, and? What's your point?" I said, sticking my chin out.

He laughed. "You lot are just completely mad," he said. "Let me guess – one of Kenny's brainwaves, was it?"

"It was kind of everybody's idea," I said defensively. "The metal detector was going off all over the bowling green when we tried it, so..." I shrugged.

"Tom! Lyndsey is busy cleaning right now so let her get on with it, please," came my mum's sharp voice. She came into the bathroom looking cross and flustered. "Has either of you two seen my watch?" she said, looking behind the soap dish and in the medicine cabinet. "I can't find it anywhere."

"No," Tom and I chorused in surprise. Mum is quite an organised person and doesn't usually lose her things around the house. That's my job!

"I know I took it off before I went to clean the front windows," Mum said, frowning. "But it's whether I took it off in the kitchen while I filled up the bucket or if I took it off outside..." A thought struck her and she tutted crossly. "Oh – I bet I left it on the front windowsill. Yes, I'm sure I did now I think about it. I just hope it's still there..."

She rushed out of the bathroom suddenly, and Tom and I followed. I knew she was thinking about the thief who'd been stealing jewellery from under people's noses. And if that watch had been pinched, Mum was going to be absolutely gutted. It was a small, silver antique watch that had been passed down through the family from her grandmother and Mum had had it restored recently. I don't know much about watches but from the way Mum looked after it, I reckon it must have been worth loads.

The three of us went outside to look for it – but we were too late. The windowsills had a few soapsuds left on them but that was all. Nothing else. We looked up and down the road but no one was there. The thief had struck again – and vanished just as mysteriously as ever, this time with Mum's watch.

Mum's face was like thunder as she shook her head in disbelief. "No," she said. "It's gone. I can't believe it. Someone has had the cheek to come right up to the house and take it – almost from under my nose! But who?"

CHAPTER TEN

Lunch time was just about the most miserable meal I've ever sat through. Not only was I still in deep do-do with Mum and Dad after the treasure-hunting disaster, but now Mum was really upset and angry about her watch being stolen. Normally, Saturday lunches are really fun and jolly, but this one... phew. Talk about a bad atmosphere... I hardly dared open my mouth.

After lunch, Mum called the police to report her missing watch, but, judging from her mood afterwards, they weren't very helpful.

"It's hopeless!" she grumbled when she came back into the kitchen. (I was in there washing up the lunch things.) "Well, I won't be seeing that watch again, if those slow coaches down at the station are leading the search. Honestly! It took him five minutes to get our address written down properly. No wonder the thief hasn't been caught yet." She slumped into a chair looking fed up.

"Do you want me to make you a cup of tea, Mum?" I asked timidly. The mood she was in, I was nervous she'd bite my head off for speaking, but she gave me a little smile instead.

"That would be lovely, darling," she said. "Thank you. Although the day I'm having, I'm tempted to have a gin and tonic instead. JOKE," she added as I hesitated at the kettle, not sure if she was serious. She sighed and stood up. "Do you fancy helping me make some bread this afternoon? Maybe a bit of dough pounding will clear up my bad mood."

"Yeah, of course," I said. I was quite keen to help clear up her bad mood, too, so that I didn't get the brunt of it!

We'd just started getting the ingredients out, when Mum groaned. "We're out of yeast. Could you run down to the shop and get me a packet, please?"

My eyes lit up. Cool – maybe Mum had changed her mind about me going out! Maybe she was so worked up about her missing watch that she'd forgotten I was on planet grounded. "Does this mean..." I began cautiously.

"No, you're still grounded," she replied at once, reading my mind. (How do mums manage to do that?) "You can go to the shop and that's it – and if you're not back in ten minutes, I will come out and find you!"

"OK, OK," I said hurriedly, pulling my trainers on and making a run for it before she could change her mind.

For the hundredth time, I wished we'd never gone near the stupid bowling green. Stupid digging! Stupid metal detector! Stupid bowling team! My weekend had been ruined! I wondered how the rest of the Sleepover gang were getting on. Probably about as miserably as I was. Probably all up to their eyes in housework like me. Suddenly, the thought of going to school on Monday was quite appealing – and it's not often you hear me say THAT.

Things were about to get even worse, though, believe it or not. The shop was quite busy and there was a long queue of people. When it was finally my turn to be served, I handed over the packet of dried yeast only for Mrs Jones, who works there at weekends, to grab my hand over the counter. "That's my Lisa's ring you're wearing!" she said loudly. "How did you get hold of that, eh?"

It was one of those moments where you just wish the ground would open up and swallow you. Everyone in the queue behind me suddenly went quiet and I knew they were earwigging. Somebody tutted and somebody else started whispering. I heard the word "thief" and I was filled with horror. I went bright red in the face, right up to my ears.

"It was in our g-g-garden," I stammered. "Buster dug it up... it was under our ash tree."

"Really?" said Mrs Jones sarcastically, raising an eyebrow. I could tell she didn't believe me for a second. "Well, I think I'll have that back, thank you," she added, holding her hand out. "My Lisa is very fond of that ring!"

I scrabbled to get the ring off and dropped it into her open palm. "Honestly, Mrs Jones, I'm not the thief," I said, paying for the yeast as quickly as possible. "I swear I'm not! My mum's watch has gone missing, too, you know!"

"Maybe I should have a look for our Vera's bracelet under the Collins's tree, what do you reckon?" came a low voice from behind me.

"And my Nick's watch," someone else said.

Cheeks flaming, I grabbed the yeast and my change, and ran out of the shop, not daring to look anyone in the face. I felt soooo awful. Everyone in there thought that it had been ME who had gone round stealing things. Me, the thief!

For the second time that day, I burst into tears as I ran back home. Little Wearing is such a small, gossipy village that it would only take a few hours for the word to get round – Lyndsey Collins is the thief! She's the one!

But of course, I WASN'T. I wouldn't dream of stealing anything!

I was really sobbing by the time I got back home and Mum looked quite startled when she opened the front door. "What's happened?" she said. "Did you fall over?"

"No!" I wailed. I almost wished that I had when she said that – wished that I was crying about something that could be sorted out as easily as a grazed knee.

I sobbed out the whole story and she put her arm around me. "Oh, Lyndz," she said sympathetically. "How horrible."

"That woman's got a nerve," Dad said, who'd heard the whole thing. I was crying so loudly the whole street had probably heard, to be honest. "How dare she accuse you?"

"Everyone's going to think I'm the thief," I wailed, and Mum hugged me tighter.

"No, they're not," she said. "Not if I've got anything to do with it, they won't. We'll put the record straight. I'll go down to that shop myself and tell Mrs Jones – and the whole village, if I have to!"

"Don't you worry, love," Dad said, patting my back. "We'll get it sorted out. There must be some kind of mistake."

I was still feeling gutted. "We DID find the ring in our garden, ask the others!" I sobbed. "They know that I'm not lying."

"We know that you're not lying, as well," Mum said, "but we've got to get to the bottom of this. How did Lisa's ring end up in our garden?"

"Let's get the other girls round," Dad suggested. "I know they're all grounded but this is getting out of hand. We can't have the village saying that our Lyndz is the thief."

"Good idea," Mum said, grabbing the phone. "What's Frankie's number, Lyndz? I'll give her mum a ring – and the others. If we all get our heads together, we might be able to work it all out."

"Especially with the mighty Sleepover Club on the case!" Dad said.

I managed a smile at that. It was true, though – we'd solved a few mysteries before. It was definitely worth a try.

Mum phoned the other parents to tell them what had happened, and they all agreed to come round to help with the puzzle.

The Sleepover gang hugged me when they arrived. "Don't worry, Lyndz, we're on the case now," Frankie said.

"Yeah, we'll find a way to prove you're not the thief," Kenny vowed.

"OK, girls, show us again where Buster found the ring," Mum said, when everyone had arrived.

We all walked out into the garden and the five of us pointed out the spot where Buster's nose had first found the ring. It seemed a long time ago now, after all the treasure hunting we'd done.

"Maybe the thief dropped it as he was running through the gardens from Mrs Brody's house," Dad said.

"If that were the case, he or she would have come from this side, is that right?"

Kenny's dad asked, pointing to the right side of the garden.

"Yes, over that fence," Mum told him.

Mr McKenzie went to have a look at the fence, to see if there were any signs of it being kicked or knocked as the thief had gone over it. The rest of us stayed under the tree, thinking as hard as we could. Just as my brain was starting to ache, there was a rustling of leaves and a loud chittering noise from above.

"That bloomin' magpie," Dad said. "Likes to make his presence felt, that one." Then he stopped suddenly and looked thoughtfully at my mum. "Hang on a minute," he said slowly. "I wonder if..." He stopped, and looked up into the branches. "Here, what's that old magpie got in his beak?"

The rest of us strained our eyes up to see. "Looks like a bit of silver foil or something," Rosie said distractedly. "But what's that got to do with..."

Mum laughed and clapped her hand to her mouth suddenly. "Of course!" she said. "I bet you're right, Keith."

Rosie's mum was smiling, too, as if she was in on the joke. "Yes, of course," she said. "We should have guessed!"

I stared at them, and then at the other Sleepover girls. Were we missing something here? What were they driving at?

"Silver foil?" Fliss repeated, looking as blank as me. "What's that got to do with anything?"

Dad went off to get a ladder from the shed. "Let's have a look in the old boy's nest, shall we?" he said with a grin.

We were all still confused but Mum explained. "Magpies love bright, shiny things," she said. "I bet you anything that it's the magpie who's the village thief – the one who took Mrs Brody's bracelet and my watch and Lisa's ring."

I gawped at her but suddenly it was starting to make sense. "And maybe he dropped the ring when he was on his way back to the nest," I said. "And the necklace we found. The cheeky old thing!"

Dad climbed up the ladder and sure enough, when he got to the top and peered into the nest, he gave a shout of triumph. "Look at this lot!" he said, pulling out one treasure after another. The missing bracelet, Mum's watch, someone's necklace, a couple of pieces of silver foil, some shiny coins...

We all stared open-mouthed. "That nest is practically a treasure chest in itself!" Mum said, shaking her head in disbelief. She put her watch back on and lovingly polished the face with the cuff of her shirt sleeve. "The crafty bird! We'd better make sure all this booty is returned – with a trip to Mrs Jones first of all. Coming?"

I felt nervous at the thought of facing angry Mrs Jones again, but Mum insisted I went along with her. In fact, all of the Sleepover Club came too! "She owes you an apology, and I'll make sure you get it," Mum said. "Come on – let's go before she has a chance to tell the whole village that she thinks you're the thief."

Mum was brilliant in the shop. She explained what had happened very loudly so that everyone could hear, and then it was Mrs Jones's turn to go red in the face and apologise. And then we went round to give all the other things back to their real owners, too.

The rest of the gang had to go back home then. "Don't think this means you're not grounded any more," Fliss's mum said warningly.

"Same goes for the rest of you," said Frankie's mum. "We might have solved the magpie mystery but you're all still in trouble over the bowling green."

"Big trouble," Kenny's dad said. "Let's go back home and see if your mum's got any more chores lined up for you, Laura."

We all groaned. Our parents were never going to let us live this down, were they? Still, at least we had found some missing treasure now – and we'd solved the mystery of the village thief. Not bad going, even if we had a bowling-green nightmare thrown into the mix, too! As I said before, the Sleepover Club rules!

All the same, I had the feeling that we would be giving treasure hunting a miss from now on. How would we ever manage to compete with the bright-eyed magpie in our garden?!

This is Lyndsey Collins, Sleepover Clubber and top treasure hunter, signing off. Over and out!

Sleepover Girls Go Snowboarding

Kenny's getting starry-eyed about her new mate Nick, a snowboarding whizz who works at the sports shop. Nothing less than a trip to the local snowboarding centre is called for! But is Nick all he's cracked up to be...?

Pack up your sleepover kit and head for the slopes!

41

The Sleepover Club at the Carnival

Carnival is coming to Cuddington! Frankie and her mates do loads of research for their carnival float – and things get seriously interesting when they stumble on some old wartime photos of the village. Who's that girl, the one who looks exactly like Kenny? Is it coincidence, or could they be related?

Dress yourself up and groove on over!

Order Form

To order direct from the publishers, just make a list of the titles you want and fill in the form below:

Name ....

Address ....

....

....

Send to: Dept 6, HarperCollins Publishers Ltd, Westerhill Road, Bishopbriggs, Glasgow G64 2QT.

Please enclose a cheque or postal order to the value of the cover price, plus:

UK & BFPO: Add £1.00 for the first book, and 25p per copy for each additional book ordered.

Overseas and Eire: Add £2.95 service charge. Books will be sent by surface mail but quotes for airmail despatch will be given on request.

A 24-hour telephone ordering service is available to holders of Visa, MasterCard, Amex or Switch cards on 0141- 772 2281.

An imprint of HarperCollins*Publishers*